Christmas
Collection

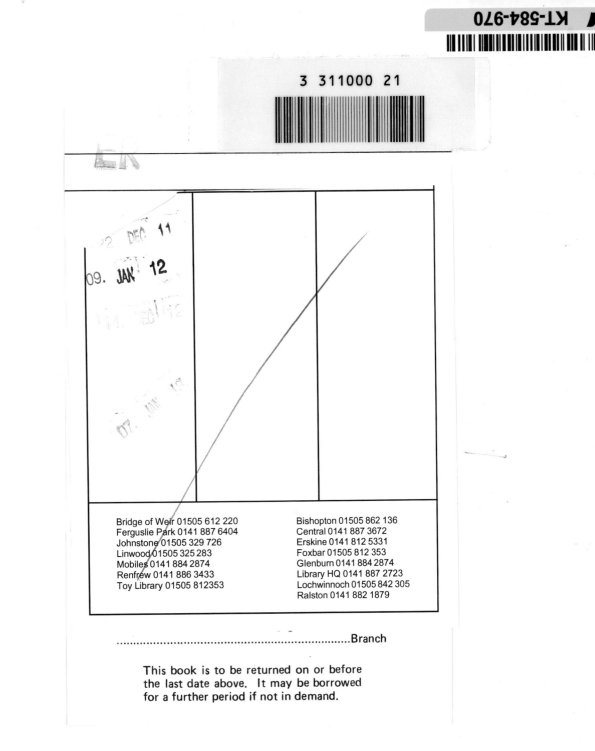

Bridge of Weir 01505 612 220 Ferguslie Park 0141 887 6404 Johnstone 01505 329 726 Linwood 01505 325 283 Mobiles 0141 884 2874 Renfrew 0141 886 3433 Toy Library 01505 812353	Bishopton 01505 862 136 Central 0141 887 3672 Erskine 0141 812 5331 Foxbar 01505 812 353 Glenburn 0141 884 2874 Library HQ 0141 887 2723 Lochwinnoch 01505 842 305 Ralston 0141 882 1879	

....Branch

This book is to be returned on or before
the last date above. It may be borrowed
for a further period if not in demand.

For Bryony Blakeway - H.O.
And her mum and dad - T.R.

3 3110 0 0 2 1

First published in Great Britain by Andersen Press Ltd in 1995
First published in Picture Lions in 1997

3 5 7 9 10 8 6 4 2

ISBN: 0 00 664596 8

Picture Lions is an imprint of the Children's Division, part of HarperCollins Publishers Ltd,
77-85 Fulham Palace Road, Hammersmith, London W6 8JB.
Text copyright © Hiawyn Oram 1995
Illustrations copyright © Tony Ross 1995
The author and illustrator assert the moral right to be identified
as the author and illustrator of the work.

Printed and bound in Singapore by Imago.

a Message for Santa

Written by Hiawyn Oram
Illustrated by Tony Ross

PictureLions
An Imprint of HarperCollins*Publishers*

Once there was a little girl called Emily.

Emily loved Christmas. She loved making Christmas decorations. She loved listening to the Christmas story.

And at the thought of all the presents she might get, wrapped up and waiting to be unwrapped, her eyes shone and her legs went skipping.

But – and it was a very big but – there was also something about Christmas that made her heart sink.

That something was Santa Claus.

So, when her grandmother took her to Santa's grotto she
wouldn't look...

...and, on Christmas Eve, when she'd had her bath and put on her pyjamas, she started blocking up the chimney.

"But Santa's good and Santa's kind," said her mother.

"Not down our chimney," said Emily firmly.

"But children everywhere, all over the world, *love* Santa. And his reindeer and his magical sleigh and his YO-HO-HOs," wailed her mother.

"Not down our chimney," said Emily even more firmly.

"Very well then," said her mother, picking up the telephone. "We had better let him know... Hello, Greenland 888? Can I speak to Santa please? Oh, he's already left, has he? Ages ago. Thank you very much. Goodbye."

"There," she said, giving Emily a gingerbread snowman. "As you heard, he's already on his way. So this is what I want you to do. I want you to sit down, close your eyes and imagine *you're* Santa...

...imagine *you've* been travelling all night leaving presents for sad children and lonely children and children who have hardly any toys at all...

...and now you've arrived on our roof and you're hungry and thirsty and your reindeer are fretting and your bag isn't getting any lighter... what's the last thing in the world you need to find?"

"That I'm stuck in the chimney," said Emily from far away on the rooftops, "because it's all blocked up."

"Exactly," said her mother. "And when you do at last get unstuck you still have to heave out all the presents for our house and put them back in your sack and find someone else to give them to, like Carmen across the road…"

"All right," said Emily quickly, opening her eyes. "He can come in here. Through these doors but only up to the edge of the table and not one step further."

"Done," said her mother. And together they wrote out a message, attached it to a long piece of wire and a broom handle and stuck it up the chimney so Santa couldn't miss it.

This is what it said.

And much much later Emily heard Santa get the message.
  "WO-WO-WO," she heard him say. "This must be from someone
who isn't too sure of Santa. Someone who's maybe even *afraid*
of Santa...

...which doesn't surprise me since I myself am afraid of all sorts of things, like bad toothache and blocked up chimneys. And as this little someone has gone to all the trouble of letting me know she's not too sure of me, she had better be very carefully listened to."

Then Emily heard Santa slide off the roof, crunch down the gravel path, open the kitchen doors,

put the presents on the table, stroke the cat, eat a mince pie, write
Emily and her sister a thank you note,

and leave, not very quietly, but very cheerfully.

And in the morning, when Emily came downstairs and found that he'd done all of it without stepping one foot past the table, *exactly as he was told,*

she was so pleased that after she'd opened her presents

and eaten the last chocolate angel from the Christmas tree,

she went into a corner and dialled Santa on her brand new
telephone.

"Next year, Santa, when you get to us," she said, "you can even
take a nap on the sofa if you're tired..."

And from that day on, Emily was never afraid to say when she was frightened of things.

"Because," she explained to her sister, "everyone's afraid of something some of the time. Even Santa..."

And she read her the letter she knew off by heart, which said so..

SANTA CLAUS / NORTH POLE

Dear Emily and Katie.
Thank you for the mince pie
and drink of juice and for
not making me be stuck
in the chimney.
Yours sincerely
Until next year
Santa

Collins
Picture Lions

Have you read all these stories by Tony Ross?

😊 Listen out for these stories on tape: 😊

I Want My Potty • I Want To Be • I Want My Dinner • Reckless Ruby